Saving Faith

To Elsa,

Keep purring loudly

Susan A—

Dear Elsa,
I hope you
enjoy the
baby cat!

Saving Faith

✦

The Adventures of Baby Cat
in Cherry Grove

Tim Steffen
and
Susan Ann Thornton

illustrations
by
Susan Ann Thornton

iUniverse, Inc.
New York Lincoln Shanghai

Saving Faith
The Adventures of Baby Cat in Cherry Grove

iUniverse books may be ordered through booksellers or by contacting:

iUniverse
2021 Pine Lake Road, Suite 100
Lincoln, NE 68512
www.iuniverse.com
1-800-Authors (1-800-288-4677)

Because of the dynamic nature of the Internet, any Web addresses or links contained in this book may have changed since publication and may no longer be valid.

This is a work of fiction. All of the characters, names, incidents, organizations, and dialogue in this novel are either the products of the author's imagination or are used fictitiously.

For more information, please visit www.baby-cat.com.

ISBN: 978-0-595-46844-7 (pbk)
ISBN: 978-0-595-91136-3 (ebk)

Printed in the United States of America

This book is lovingly dedicated to
our belated and beloved
four-legged and two-legged friends.

Contents

THE BABY CAT SONG

Baby Cat …
Baby Cat …
Baby Cat …
I love my Baby Cat.

Now Baby Cat I'm here to say,
I love you each and every day,
every day and every way,
I love my Baby Cat.

And Baby Cat through thick and thin,
without you girl I'd never win.
Baby you are my best friend,
I love you Baby Cat.

Baby Cat …
Baby Cat …
Baby Cat …
I love my Baby Cat.

Baby Cat so far from home,
Baby Cat just loves to roam,
Baby Cat always comes home,
I love you Baby Cat.

Baby Cat …
Baby Cat …
Baby Cat …
I love my Baby Cat.

I am Baby Cat. I love to be Bobcat, too, which you'll find out about in this story. My moms named me Lily. I am a prowler, a meower, the queen of cat power. I can get mad, but mostly I'm glad to be where I am. I'm the happiest cat when I'm in Cherry Grove, and this is where my *second* adventure begins ...

1

WE'VE LOST FAITH!

✦

*Losing Faith
is not what we meant,
we love her completely,
one hundred percent.*

"What the meow are you talking about?" I asked the two cats
as I peered through the screen door.

"Oh dear, oh dear!" cried Romeo, the cat we all called Rome for short. "Lily! We've lost Faith!"

"Will you please close your mousetrap and let me do the talking," moaned Alfa, also known as Alf. The whiskers on his face twitched in his usual annoyance at his cat companion. The two were inseparable.

"You brute!" sobbed Rome, shaking his head.

"He's *very* sensitive," whispered Alf with a roll of his eyes.

"There's nothing wrong with that," sniffed Rome. "I've always been a bit of a delicate fragile flower, like an orchid."

Alf groaned, "More like poison ivy."

Alf and Rome, two of three cats in my troop of mouse-hunters called Lily's Pride, stood on the other side of the door. I was always amused by the way they truly loved each other one moment and the next their claws were ready to scratch a few eyes out. And now they sat at the front door of Casita with a frantic look in their eyes.

Casita was the little beach cottage where I chose to live, and Susan and Nancy were the two-leggeds I chose to live with.

That's the way it is with cats. Some of the best and smartest two-leggeds are owned by cats.

It was my third summer in Cherry Grove. Spring was over, and with it the fireplace was no longer used; the windows stayed open; the garden was in bloom with lilies; a soft breeze from the ocean tucked us in soundly to sleep every night.

It was a warm, drizzly June morning. My moms were sleeping quietly with a gently snoring Spike, the other cat that lives with me. He's okay, but he sure does sleep a lot.

Summer raindrops gently tapped on the rooftop. The water slid off the roof, down the gutters and snuck through the spaces between the boards of the deck to find a new home in the sand below.

I had just finished a late morning snack and was thinking of curling up on the bed for a nap with my family, something I love doing on a rainy day, but it seemed that other matters were now more pressing.

"How could you lose a dog?" I asked as I licked my paw and rubbed it over my cheek, pushing back my whiskers. I am a very clean kitty, especially after a delightful nibble. Susan uses the word "fastidious" to describe me. "And why would you want to live with a dog?" I added.

"Can we come in?" asked Rome.

"Not unless you can open a door," I replied.

"If only," he lamented. "Maybe we'll figure doorknobs out one of these days."

"We don't have thumbs," Alf said, annoyed once again.

"What do you mean?" asked Rome.

"Never mind."

"We didn't really lose Faith," Rome continued. He sat up on his hind legs and pushed his front paws against the screen as if that would help the situation.

Alf whisked his tail in the air. "She's not really lost," he sighed, "but she's nowhere to be found."

"Same thing," meowed Rome.

I suggested that maybe she just went out for a walk around the block.

"No, no," said Rome. "Denise said something about flying to a place called Hawaii on something called a ... vacation, and she's been gone since yesterday, along with Faith."

"Maybe she took her with her," I said.

"No, no," said Rome.

"Denise doesn't fly with her four-leggeds," Alf said.

"She left food for us," continued Rome, "but Faith is really, truly, undeniably, absolutely, without a doubt—

"—nowhere to be found," finished Alf.

Rome scratched at the screen. "Lily, we need to talk. Now!"

"We are talking," I said, "and she can't be far. We're on an island."

Rome hollered, "Well, of course she can't be far, but where the meow is she?"

I shook my head. "Why are you so worried about a dog?"

"She's not just a dog," replied Rome.

"She's our Faith," said Alf sincerely.

I couldn't understand why any cat would want to live with a four-legged creature called a dog. Even though Susan loves all four-leggeds and wing*eds*, or what you would call birds, I've heard her say, "I like dogs, but Nancy and I have chosen to live with cats."

I didn't want to deal with the boys' problem at that moment, but old Fellini would have said that I was leader of the Pride and had to come to our friends' aid when needed.

"I'll catch up with you later in the dunes," I said. "Right now I've got something else I have to do."

"Okay," sighed the boys. They seemed a little downhearted, but it wasn't my fault that Faith was missing. I had a well-deserved nap coming up, and besides, Faith could wait. Also, it was raining and I didn't want to get wet. And last of all, me and Susan had a lunch date with Maggie.

The two cats skulked away down the walk, under the gate, back into the wetness of the very early morning on the board-walks of Cherry Grove.

2

MORNING RITUALS

✦

Pitter-patter, pitter-patter,
the rain goes on for hours,
it keeps us in our homes,
but it's very good for flowers.

A little later that morning, the rain became a drizzle, the drizzle turned to mist, and the mist burned off in the rising sun to create another sparkling day in the Grove, exactly as I had asked. That's one of the many special things about Cherry Grove—the weather can change on a whisker.

"This is exactly the weather that I planned on having today," said Susan brightly as she sipped something steaming from her mug.

"Me, too," I purred.

Nancy came out of the bedroom, kissed Susan and took off for her ritual Saturday morning run in the Sunken Forest, another place I'll tell you about one of these days. It's a place where Fellini says treasure is buried.

I heard Spike jump down from the bed and saunter into the kitchen. He yawned, licked his chops, and stood by the cabinet door. Susan understood exactly what he wanted. She opened the door, reached in and scooped up some food from a large, crinkly paper bag. She poured the handful into Spike's bowl and stroked his back.

"You're always eating," I meowed.

"I'm always hungry," he mumbled. "You gotta get it while you can, kitty, and I've definitely earned it."

He bent his head and gobbled his food.

"How did you earn it?" I asked.

"You're the Baby Cat now, but when I was young, I danced on the railings, chased Carm and Tony, climbed trees, played with Cliff, and party-hopped. What have you done?"

I had no idea what he was talking about.

He sighed as he chewed. "Back in the day, every weekend there were parties galore. And at these parties was food. Hamburgers, chicken, steak, you name it."

"What's a hamburger?" I asked.

Spike shook his head and swallowed his food. "I would visit different parties and was always sure, with a cute meow and loving rub against someone's leg, to get a morsel or more of food. It was cat heaven."

"You? Spike?"

"You'll see, Lily, one of these days," he said. "Everything spreads out over time, especially age, but you can still stay young."

"I'll never get old," I chirped like a bird.

Spike gave me a rare smile. "Keep that in your hairy head and don't forget it."

Without warning, which is the way most of us kitties act, I pounced on Spike's back. He took off in a sprint across the living room and I laughed the whole way, under the table, onto the couch, into the air, and back to the floor, sliding across the tile for a grand finish smack into the food bowl, bits of cat food scattering everywhere.

"Get off of me!" he yelled. "You're too big for this kind of shenanigans."

"You said that I'll never get old!"

"That doesn't mean you don't grow bigger and heavier!" Spike let out a howl and ran around the stool. I knew he loved every minute of it. Maybe Spike wasn't so old after all.

A little later I walked around the back deck and thought about Alf and Rome and Faith. There's no way Faith could get off the island with the ocean on one side and the bay on the other. This was our sanctuary, our safe place. This was our little beach town in the middle of a barrier beach called Fire Island. It was our place to hunt, to play, to talk, to kitty kiss, to call our home.

Every kitten comes up with a certain morning routine, or as I like to call it, *my* ritual. This is a typical morning in the life of me, Lily, the Babycat, the prowler, the meower, the queen of cat power:

ONE
Give Susan and Nancy kitty kisses to get them out of bed to open the door.

"All right, Baby Cat, give us a second," they said.

I'm still working on the doorknob thing, trying to figure out what a thumb is without having to ask Alf.

TWO
Sit in the garden and make sure everything is okay.

The lilies were blooming. Did you know they were named after me? The two cardinals, Latifah and Redboy, always together, sang to each other in the Holly Tree. Redboy

grabbed a seed from one of our birdfeeders and brought it to his mate.

THREE
Attack Don's broom while he sweeps the boardwalk outside his House of Orange.

"Scat, Lily!" he yelled like always, waving his broom in the air. He sure loves to sweep.

FOUR
Make sure Dick and Buddy's garden is safe from snakes.

"What are ya up to, Lily?" asked Dick from the second floor deck. He carried a chair down the stairs. He's always doing something while Buddy's always baking.

I jumped up on the fence and onto the stair railing. Up and up I skipped until I was on the second floor. I didn't want to stop so I leaped onto the roof. I could see the wide bay and endless ocean on either side. I can climb anywhere. I walked along the roof then made my way back down to the board-walk.

"Where ya going now, Lily?" Dick asked as he put the chair down on the porch.

"To Syd's!" I meowed.

"Are you talking to yourself again?" yelled Buddy from inside. "And where's my favorite oven mit?!"

FIVE
*Jump onto Syd's railing and say good morning to him
and his tenants, Jeffrey and Craig.*

"Hello, Lily!" yelled Syd as he watered the plants on his deck.

On the other side of the house Jeffrey sat outside working on a dress with thread and needle.

"Hi Lily, I'm hemming a dress for Bella," Jeffrey said. "Wanna help?"

"Maybe later," I meowed.

One time, Jeffrey fixed a favorite pair of pants for Susan. She was happy for his help, as are most two-leggeds that come to him, especially around the Fourth of July, but that's for another story. Sometimes he likes to dress up as Empress Gefil Tefish. I don't always know it's him until I hear his soft voice.

He smiled and said, "With a stitch-stitch here, and a hem-hem there, and a couple of collars sewn, that's how I sew the day away in the merry land of the Grove!"

Craig walked out of the house with a fireman's hat on his head and waved. "Hi, Lily!"

"Hi Craig!"

Sometimes, if I'm in the mood, I'll stop and let Craig give me a back massage, but not today. Too much to do!

SIX
Stop by Bob Danskin's cottage on the bay because he really loves and understands me.

"Lily," he said, "have you seen the swans and ducks?"

I hadn't, so I followed him to his deck on the bay.

I saw the large snowy swans and the dipping, diving ducks and decided against going after big birds, especially since they lived on the water.

SEVEN

*Make my way over to the house called A to Z and say my meows
to Lana and Laura's little two-legged children, Alex and Zack.*

"Mommy, Lily's here!" they both yelled, splashing in the hot
tub. "Hi, Lily!"

"Hi kids!" I meowed back to them. They're two of the few
cute two-leggeds.

Lana and Laura walked out, said their hellos to me and
scooped the children up. "Time for the beach," they both
sang.

EIGHT

*Follow Cliff the Magic Squirrel along the fence to the back deck
and let him enjoy a quick breakfast.*

Why is he magic? I guess
because he's the only squirrel
that doesn't really bother me.
He also has the uncanny abil-
ity to know exactly what's
happening in the neighborhood at any given time.

"How are things, Cliffy?" I asked.

Cliff went flat on the railing and then saw that it was just me. He trotted over to the birdfeeder, scooped a paw full of sunflower seeds and replied, "Things are fine, Lily. Just a little nuts as usual."

NINE
Back to the front of Casita to watch Chick at the birdfeeder.

"How are things, Chick?" I asked.

The tiny wing*ed* cocked his head and chirped, "Blueberries are coming!"

I knew that meant that Nancy would be baking pies very soon.

TEN

Finally, if I'm in the mood and Susan's around, I become Bobcat.

Susan stood outside the side door and scratched the boards overhead calling, "Bobcat! Bobcat Girl!"

The three things you need to do with cats are the following: talk, listen, and, most importantly, *play*. I think play should be a part of life for every living thing.

I was Bobcat. I jumped on the bench, sprang up onto the fence, and then nimbly made my way across the trellis, high above the deck. Bobcat is also an acrobat, or "acrocat". I hopped from board to board as Mom scratched at them and then I went after her hands with my paws.

Sometimes I get a little carried away and my claws come out, but Mom understands I'm just being a kitty, so she's careful not to get too close.

I jumped onto the roof of the shed and rubbed my chin against the gutter, dangling my paws over the side, occasionally grabbing at Mom. Susan and Nancy both have different games they like to play with me. They're my best friends for a lot of reasons.

I hung out on the roof of the shed for a bit, but once I was done being Bobcat I let Mom know by climbing down and doing one of the other things I love best, lying under the bench on the back deck to take a nice, long catnap.

3

LUNCH ALA MAGGIE

✦

Lunch with a song,
lunch with a friend,
lunch all day long,
till the daylight ends.

Susan poured some food into my dish and went back to stirring the soup she was making until we heard a few taps on the door.

"Knock, knock!" said a voice.

Maggie. There's no two-legged like her in Cherry Grove, or even in the whole world, however big that is.

Sugar, my deer friend, sometimes talks of water sprites that she's seen dancing on the ocean under the moonlight. She says they're small, they look like two-leggeds, are the color of the sea, and live in the water. That's how I would describe Maggie, but I don't think she lives in the water.

Susan hugged Maggie like a very good friend would do.

"Hiya, Honey," Maggie said.

She stroked my head. "How ya doin', Sweety?"

I purred all over.

One of the many, many things I can share with you about cats is how we communicate with you. Cats understand two-legged talk, we just can't speak it. A few two-leggeds can even understand us cats, like Maggie and Susan.

One of the ways we communicate with you is by purring. A purr can mean many things, just like a smile on a two-legged doesn't always mean she's happy. You just have to listen carefully to cats. Here are a few kinds of purrs you should know about:

1. A happy purr. Prrrrr ...

2. An upset purr. Prrrrr ...

3. A getting ready for a nap purr. Prrrrr ...

4. A snoring purr. Prrrrr ...

5. A friendly purr. Prrrrr …

They all sound the same, right? But, they're not and there are many more. If you can listen well and learn these purrs, you'll be a cat's best friend.

Susan and Maggie ate their soup and talked about the Grove while I lay on top of the sofa and listened with half-closed eyes. I could see Nancy's feet on the bed through the bedroom door. She was probably napping. She's very much like a cat sometimes, especially Spike.

"What do you say to a walk in the woods?" asked Susan as she cleared the dishes.

I whisked my tail hopefully. Susan had talked about it, but I had never been in the woods. I had merely staked my territory between Aeon and Ivy Walks, which was only four boardwalk blocks—not much to meow about.

"I say it sounds great," said Maggie with a nod of her head.

Susan opened the door and I sprung onto the railing. I walked lightly towards the gate when I heard a sudden flutter around my ears. Something nipped at my rear end. I meowed angrily and looked up to see Carm, the blue jay, land on the wire above my head. Tony sat beside her and the two laughed that awful blue jay laugh that gives me big tail.

What's big tail? Big tail is anytime a cat's tail hair stands on its ends. It either puffs up in anger, annoyance, fear, or all of the above. Big tail sends a clear signal to anyone around that you are not dealing with a calm kitty. She is *totally* freaked out!

"Hey Carm," chirped Tony.

"What?" asked Carm.

"Did you hear about the cat who swallowed a ball of wool?"

Carm ruffled her wings. "No, I didn't."

"She had mittens," Tony screamed.

They squawked and I ming-minged.

"She's ming-minging," I heard Susan say from behind me.

"What's that?" asked Maggie.

"It's when Lily goes 'ming-ming."

Maggie looked at me and nodded. "So she's annoyed?"

Susan nodded. "To say the least."

You don't want to get near me when I ming-ming.

Carm jumped up in the air, shook her wings, and landed on the other side of Tony.

"Hey, Tony," she said long and loud.

"What?" he asked.

"What does a cat that lives near the beach have in common with Christmas?"

"I don't know," replied Tony.

"Sandy claws!" screamed Carm.

They squawked. I ming-minged again. As Maggie would say, I was annoyed.

Quicker than a flea in a mouse ear Tony swooped down and went for my tail, but I was quick and batted my paw at him. I barely missed the little blue bugger as Carm dove from the other side. We both missed each other, but I was very close to grabbing her wing, so close that a blue feather floated silently in front of my nose. I swatted it away and glared at the two winged*s* above me, totally out of reach. *Ming-ming.*

"Did you see that?" Maggie said with a big laugh.

"Happens every day," said Susan with a shrug of her shoulders.

As Carm and Tony flew away, another joke faded from my ears.

"Hey Carm, why did the cat run away from the tree?"

The two birdbrains flitted over the trees, out of sight, out of mind.

However, we happy three passed through the gate, down the walk, making a right paw turn onto Bayview Walk. We made our course towards the unfamiliar place at the end of the walk that my two friends called *the woods*.

4

INTO THE WOODS

✦

Into the woods,
we're going to play,
all sorts of games,
all through the day.

"Yay, Lily! Yay!" said Warren as he walked out of the woods and raised his hands. He stopped at the end of the walk between two benches and high stalks of bamboo. He was one of Susan's two-legged friends who was a guest at Casita on many Sundays. He and Nancy always played a game called *Scrabble*.

"Hi, Susan, hi Maggie," he said as he bent down. He touched my head and asked, "And what kind of adventure are you going on today?"

"Into the woods," said Susan. "Like a kitty ... romping for the very first time."

Warren smiled so wide I thought his chin was going to fall off and bounce into the bay. "Yay, Lily! Yay!" he yelled and clasped his hands together. "Your first time in the woods!" He patted me on the head again and stood up. His hands always tell me that Warren is a good one, like most of my moms' friends.

"One of these days, Lily, you'll come with me on a Moon-walk," he said. "There's lots of fireflies and moonlight and *magic.*"

"Maybe we should invite Cliff," I said as Warren's footsteps faded away.

At the end of the boardwalk two steps led down to the sand and grass of the woods. It was thick with bushes, trees, and roots bursting out of the sand. Narrow paths went here and there and everywhere.

Susan and Maggie walked past me and stepped softly onto the sand and patches of moss. They both turned back and stared at me for a moment, Susan's hands on her hips.

I stared back at them, not moving. I had never been farther than Ivy Walk.

"Lily," said Susan, "if you want to come with us, you need to stay with us."

"Okay," I meowed, but stood my place.

"Maybe she's not ready," said Susan.

"Listen, Honey," began Maggie with a raised eyebrow, "she's ready." She waved her hand at me. "Come on, Lily. It's time."

They both turned and entered the woods. There was a *purrfectly* good bowl of food back at the house. Maybe I should check in on my Pride in the dunes. Maybe Monroe the Mouse had some new little tidbit of gossip for me. I had also promised to play with Sugar. Cliff the Magic Squirrel was always good for some fun. I should go where I'm safe and happy. That's what I'll do, I'll—

"Lily," called Maggie from somewhere inside the woods. It wasn't a command, but it wasn't a request. It was somewhere in between.

I stopped thinking and moved one paw in front of the other. I guess it wasn't that creepy after all. I kept going, a little faster with each paw, eyes straight ahead until I was inside the woods next to Maggie and Susan.

Trees, trees everywhere. Straight trees, knobby, knotty trees, twisting, curling, whirling trees that lifted their branches into a big umbrella over our heads. Sandy paths going this way and that. Wing*eds* flitting, chirping. A little bridge over swampy ground. And air. Crisp, fresh air pushed from the ocean through the trees. The lapping of water on the bayside. The crash of the waves on the ocean side. Surrounded by it all.

Maggie knew how to play with a little kitty like me. She picked up a stick, let me sniff it, and then threw it up the path. I stood still.

"It's okay, Baby Cat," said Susan. "Go get the stick if you want to."

"Don't you wanna get it?" asked Maggie. She has a way of asking that just makes you want to do it.

"Don't get lost," added Susan.

I whisked my tail and put my nose up. "I'd never get lost," I meowed. "I know how to smell my way around any old place."

I ran ahead toward the stick and pushed it with my nose. I turned back, but Maggie and Susan were gone. I wasn't scared, of course. A kitty is never scared, especially in a place like the woods. There was nothing to be scared of. Wait. What was that noise? It was a scraping noise, like a giant pair of cat claws scratching across a tree. I looked up and saw a branch rubbing against another branch in the breeze. I knew it was only that. I wasn't a scaredy cat.

"Susan?" I meowed. "Maggie?" I waited. Nothing. And then I heard a familiar voice.

"We're right here, Baby Cat," Susan said as the two of them walked around a bend in the path.

"I knew you were," I said and ran over to them, trying not to seem too relieved.

We continued around the winding path of sand, walking across the light blanket of pine needles until I came to a tree that looked perfect to climb. I had never climbed a tree, but I suddenly had the urge to do it like Spike used to do. I walked around it, looked up—*lots of branches*, I thought.

Susan said, "I know you can climb, Baby Cat, but if you go up there, you're going to have to get down. Do you know how to get down?"

"Of course I do," I meowed.

"It's not the same as climbing around Dick and Buddy's house."

Maggie piped up, "She'll figure it out."

I wrapped my paws around the tree trunk, dug in my claws, and climbed up easily. I jumped from branch to branch and almost lost hold, but my claws were strong and sharp. Then I made the mistake of looking down.

"Come on girl!" Susan exclaimed.

"You can do it!" Maggie called.

From my high perch they both looked like dune mice, but without the tails.

I guess sometimes you're on your own and have to figure things out, but it was nice to have a cheering crowd below. *Very* far below.

I couldn't go headfirst. I'd fall head over tail. I figured there was no other way down but the way I came, so once again I wrapped my paws around the tree and backed down slowly, carefully until I was close enough to jump down into the sand.

"Way to go, Sweety!" yelled Maggie.

"Much easier than doorknobs," I said with a slight bow of my head.

We looped around and started to make our way back to the Grove.

I was startled by a rustling behind a bush. It was Sugar! My friend the doe.

"Hi Sugar!" I yelled.

"Lily!" Sugar said with a mouthful of leaves. "So you're coming to the woods now?"

"My first time," I said.

"Hi Sugar," Maggie said from behind us.

I turned and twitched my whiskers. How did Maggie know Sugar?

Sugar bobbed her head towards Maggie. "Hello, Maggie."

"You two know each other?" I meowed.

"Sugar and I go way back," Maggie said.

"That's true," Sugar said.

"I know a lot of animals," said Maggie. "Deer, squirrels, birds, cats, dogs, don't I Susan?"

"You bet."

I meowed, "Dogs?"

"She's quite a pip," Maggie laughed.

Susan seemed to know what I was thinking. "Dogs are nice, Sweety. I like dogs, but Nancy and I—"

"—have chosen to live with cats," I finished.

"Lily," said Maggie, "in all my years I've never known any strangers. It's okay to be friendly."

Hmm, I'd have to think about that later. Right then I wanted to play with Sugar. I think Sugar knew what I was thinking because she bent down her head and bumped me on my rear end. It was time for *Sugar Bumps*! I jumped up in the air and ran to the right. She came after me and bumped me again. I ran to the left. Bumped again! And so on as we played all the way back to the Grove.

Maggie and Susan watched with delight as streams of midday sun shone through the branches and leaves. It was one of those days that I would call perfect in every way.

We arrived where we had begun our adventure and Sugar left us. The wind changed directions and began blowing in from the bay. With it came flies from the land across the way. I climbed up a tree to get a better view. Suddenly there were strange wing*eds* flying around. Bigger than flies, but smaller than birds. They were quick like lightning during a summer storm, darting here and there and everywhere. I batted at one that got too close to me.

"Don't do that, Honey," Maggie said.

"What are they?" I asked.

Maggie looked at the swarm of creatures in the air around us. "They're dragonflies, sweetheart. They take care of the flies that bite us. You should never kill a dragonfly."

I saw the dragonflies catching the pesky flies and eating them. *Oh,* I thought, *that's good, but they better stay away from me.*

Maggie watched them with an unmistakable joy. "You wanna know something?"

"What?" me and Susan said together.

"When the day comes that I have to leave the Grove, I'm gonna turn into a dragonfly. That will be a thrill."

I meowed that I didn't want Maggie to go.

"We all have to leave one of these days," she said as she stared out across the bay. "Don't we, Susan?"

Susan nodded her head and said, "But not too soon, I hope."

Dark clouds swirled together over the land across the bay. The wind picked up around us.

"Girls," Maggie said softly, "storm's comin'."

5

WHAT THE MEOW?!

✦

What the meow?!
is what we cats say,
when we don't understand,
why you don't want to play.

"Faith is still missing," said Alf when I got back to the house.

He and Rome waited for me by the gate.

"It's a terrible loss, oh, quite terrible," wailed Rome. "I would climb up a string to the moon to have our dear dog come home with us."

"Oh, stop going on so," complained Alf. "Strings to the moon! She's our dog and I want her back. Now."

"Guys," I said, trying to stop them.

Rome narrowed his eyes. "I am *not* going on, I'm just expressing my feelings, something you know nothing about."

"Guys," I said a little longer and louder.

Alf cocked his head. "I know how to express my feelings. I say what I want, no fishbones about it."

"You're a catty cat," Rome cried.

"Guys!" I shouted. "I've got some other things to do right now. Faith can't get off the island. I'm sure she's fine. We'll work out a plan in the dunes. Meet me there later."

I could tell they weren't too happy about that, but I had very important things to do, the first order of business being another well-deserved nap.

As they left, trotting forlornly down the walk towards the gate, I heard them go at it again.

"You just want Faith back so you can boss her around," said Rome.

"No, I've got you for that," Alf said.

"You just try, you dog rump."

"Scaredy cat."

"Dirty litter head!"

"Catnip brain!"

After my nap I held true to my word and went to the dunes for our daily meeting of my Pride. The usual list of events was some games and a mouse hunt.

Along the way I saw Walter and his odd dog Quetsch. Walter had the dog's leash in one hand and a bag in the other. I knew that inside this bag was what many in the Grove called the famous "Walter Cake". Always a smile, always generous, always with Quetsch by his side, Walter walked the walks and delivered his cakes to his friends, leaving them outside the door, in a mailbox, or just inside a gate.

"Well, hi, Lily," said Walter.

"Hi Walter," I said, and then looked at Quetsch. I guess I could try to be friendly. "Hi, Quetsch," I meowed every so quietly.

As usual, Quetsch ignored me, didn't say a word, and continued on his way with Walter. What a rude dog!

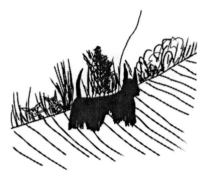

After that, it was like a dog parade! I jumped down off the walk into the sand and watched Joan and Lorraine walk by with Molly. Behind them was little Felix with his two-legged, Josh, who had been to our house a few times. I heard that Felix was something called a Chihuahua. And then there was Perry leading Jim and Robert down Louis Walk.

Dogs, dogs, dogs!

When I was finally in the rolling sandy hills, up to my nose in dune grass, I found Fellini waiting. That old, fat gray cat raised one eye sharply and said, "When I was leader of the Pride, we used to meet earlier, and every cat was on time and present."

I thought, *well, it's not your pride anymore is it, big boy*, but something held my kitty tongue from speaking too quickly. Is this what it meant to be friendly?

"Why's that dog Questch so weird?" I asked. "Every time I say hi to him, he ignores me."

"He's not ignoring you, Lily," said Fellini. "He's deaf and he can't see too well. He's an old dog. Things aren't always as they seem, Miss Kitty."

I thought, *how was I supposed to know Quetsch was deaf?* "Where's Alf and Rome?" I asked, a little annoyed.

"They're not down here," Fellini replied. "Let's go up top. I'm sure they'll be along soon."

As we walked through the tufts of grass to the top of the dune I thought about Alf and Rome. I knew where they were. I knew they were out looking for their dog. Wouldn't they rather be here with Fellini and me, with the Pride? Catching mice to munch on later?

"What's so special about living with a dog?!" I said out loud, but didn't mean to.

"What are you talking about?" asked Fellini.

I sighed. "I know where the boys are."

Fellini's tail went up in the air. "Where?"

"Looking for Faith. She's been gone for two days and they can't find her."

Fellini's tail batted at the ground. "And we haven't been helping? If I had known I would have done something."

My whiskers twitched. "Done what?"

Fellini took a deep breath and sat down on the dune. He looked out across the crystal quartz beach and swelling ocean. "I wonder how far it goes."

Oh no, I thought, *not another one of his questions that had no answer.* "What?" I asked. "The big puddle or the big sandbox?"

Fellini lifted his nose. "The puddle. Yes, I wonder if it goes on forever."

"I don't know," I said, because I really didn't know. I wasn't even sure how far or long forever was.

He sniffed at the air. "Maybe it does, maybe it doesn't. Who knows, but there's one thing I do know, Lily, and that's the love that Alf and Rome have for Faith. *That* goes on forever."

"But why do they love her so much?"

"Why do you love Susan and Nancy?"

I thought about the many, many reasons why I loved my moms. I told him that I could go on forever.

"Then if you know love, you have to trust those two cats and their love for Faith. You asked what's so special about living with a dog." Fellini turned his head toward me. "I live with a dog."

I looked into Fellini's face, stunned. "You? What the meow?!"

"Yes, and there he is right now on the beach. His name's Jimmy. My moms got him last winter and he's very nice, very sweet. Would you like to meet him?"

"You never said anything about him," I said.

"You never asked," quipped Fellini.

I looked down from the dune to the beach where a funny-looking little dog was walking with Lucy and Diane.

Fellini was an old cat, at least old compared to my age (I'm almost two). Last summer I had outwitted him to become leader of the Pride, but I thought there were still a few things I could learn from him. Maybe.

"Okay, Fellini, let's go."

Another thing I love to do is run across the beach, or gallop, as Susan calls it. I bounced around while Fellini walked. The sand made my legs spring, like walking on a bouncy bed.

Jimmy was thrilled to see us. His big ears stood up straight. His nose looked like it was pushed into his face. His cheeks drooped under lively, sparkling eyes.

"Fellini! Fellini! Come play with me!" Jimmy yipped.

"Oh, I'm too old for that, Jimmy. Why don't you play with Lily?"

"I've heard about you," barked Jimmy, looking at me. He jumped up and down.

I still wasn't convinced that dogs could be friends with cats, at least not with me.

"What kind of dog are you?" I asked.

"I'm a French Bulldog," said Jimmy, "but I have no idea what that means, do you?"

"It sounds like you're French and a Bulldog," I said. "And I have no idea what that means either."

Jimmy laughed. Maybe dogs weren't so bad. *What was I saying?!* Lily, get your head on straight!

I left Fellini with his family and walked back towards the dunes. On my way Glen and Roland passed me with the biggest puppy in the Grove—Cleo.

"Hi, Lily!" yelled Glen, the happiest and oldest two-legged in Cherry Grove. "Look how big you're getting!"

"Hi, Glen," I meowed.

Cleo was just as happy as Glen and pulled on the leash as hard as she could to get near me. Roland lunged forward with each tug.

"Lily!" she barked. "You wanna eat sand with me?! You wanna chase a ball?! You wanna chase tails?!"

Roland, who was doing his best to hold onto the leash yelled with a laugh, "Cleo! Cleo!"

"No thanks," I yelled and scurried away up the dune and down the other side. All the while I thought about how the meow Fellini and Jimmy got along so well. I thought about the way Alf and Rome loved Faith. They missed her terribly.

Alone again, I thought. I might just have to hunt mice by myself, but then I decided there was really only one mouse I needed to find, the one who I always promised to protect as long he was my spy. He is the mouse who is my eyes, my ears when I'm not there.

"Monroe?" I called pleasantly. "Oh … Monrooooooe?"

I called a few more times and then heard a crunch of grass from behind me. I sniffed the air and got down low, waited, and then pounced.

"Gotcha!" I yelled.

"I let you get me!" Monroe squeaked from underneath my paws.

I released him. He looked around nervously. "I wouldn't want any mouse to see us together. I'd be a joke for the rest of my life, your hairiness."

"The same with me," I said. "And don't call me that."

"How about exulted one?" he asked.

"Stop it and listen. Monroe, you have to help me."

He brushed the sand from his brown fur, knocked some of it out from his white-tipped ears, and pulled at his whiskers to straighten them out. "Oh wise and noble leader, what can a good-hearted little thing like myself do for such a beast, I mean, beauty as you?"

"Stop it," I said crossly. "I need information."

"You could ask nicely. A please would be nice, but spill it anyway," he said in his usual speedy voice.

"A dog is missing. I need to find her."

Monroe smiled a sly smile only he could make. "*You* want to find a dog? *You*, Lily, leader of the Pride? What the squeak are you talking about? I thought you couldn't stand dogs! I thought they were the smallest object of your affection, the drudgery of your existence, the thorn in your side, the bitter root, the skullduggery of your aggravation with all that is wrong in the world, the—"

"—they annoy me," I said with a half-smile.

Monroe's face looked at me humorously.

"Now listen," I said, "her name is Faith. She's black, about the size of Fellini."

"Sounds like a well-fed dog, your grace." Monroe never missed a beat.

"Well, not that big, just about as high and long as him. Got it?"

"Got it, boss," he squeaked.

"Don't call me that, or your grace either."

"I could think of many other things to call you," he said with a tiny mischievous wink.

"My moms call me Baby Cat, my friends call me Lily."

"Well," he said, "what am I, friend or foe?"

"You decide," I said.

6

THUNDER AT THE CATNIP CAFÉ

✦

Thunder, lightning,
crash, bang, boom!
Storms always end,
but never too soon.

The grey clouds turned darker and slowly drifted over the bay towards the Grove. How quickly things change. The sky softly rumbled. Some force was getting stronger in those clouds. I thought that maybe Maggie was right with her forecast.

I galloped down Maryland Walk towards Casita where I thought I might find Alf and Rome.

At the beginning of the season, in very early spring, we cats all decided to make our very own place where we could drink dirty water and munch on mice. A place we could go to at night or during a storm. A place protected and hidden. Fellini wanted to call it *Fellini's Joint,* but we all agreed on *The Catnip Café* and, without my moms knowing, we made it in the sand right under Casita.

Another important thing about cats you should know is that water out of a bowl is boring. It's okay for emergencies, but the rest of the time, forget it. The really cool, hip cats drink dirty water from birdbaths and puddles. The only water from a bowl we *purrfer* is toilet water.

I found Alf and Rome complaining to each other, lapping up some water from a puddle under the deck. There were oyster and mussel shells scattered around, pieces of old deck we used as seats, and an old boat that was purrfect for a game of Cat-and-Seek. There were also little bits of things that we found in the neighborhood or took from our homes like a few bouncy balls, a sachet of catnip, and fuzzy old chewed-up mouse toys. It was our very own place.

"I still think you're a catty cat," Rome meowed.

"Catty?"

"Yes … mean, malicious, malevolent. I'm never going to talk to you again."

Alf smiled. "You've been saying that for years."

Rome narrowed his eyes. "Well, now I'm going to stick to my word."

"Start sticking then," said Alf, quite amused.

"I'm starting right now."

"Now?"

"Yes."

"But you're still talking."

Rome's hair bristled. "If you'd stop talking I'd be able to shut my mousetrap."

Alf shrugged. "So shut your trap."

"I will when I'm good and ready."

"Good."

"Good."

I heard a "psst" from behind me. Monroe waved his paw from around a thick round post. I quietly slinked over to him.

"I got news, queenie," Monroe whispered.

"Good news I hope ... and don't call me that."

He looked around, darted his eyes this way and that. A single whisker twitched nervously. "I know where Faith is."

"Spill it," I said.

Monroe frowned.

I rolled my eyes and said, "Please?" Maybe it wasn't so hard to be friendly sometimes.

"Okay, I heard from Sugar who heard from Latifah and Red-boy who heard from Cliff who heard from his cousin Rocky on the West Side that Faith is definitely still on the island, and in the Grove, too."

"Where?" I asked.

"The dog saw Faith go into Amelia's house the other day."

"Who's Amelia?"

"Beats the fleas off of me. That's the news, oh clever one."
The same whisker twitched again as he sniffed the air.
"Storm's comin'." He looked at me and smiled slyly. "See ya
around ... Lily." And with that he scurried away under the
boardwalks, under the feet of two-leggeds who probably
never thought that there was all this life, all this activity going
on under their flip-flops.

"Always have to get the last word in don't you?" Alf asked as I
returned to their tussle.

"No, you do," Rome argued.

"No, I don't."

"You just did."

"No, you just did," Alf said slowly.

"Now you did!" Rome yelled.

"Never." Alf quietly licked his paw.

"Oh!" Rome shrieked.

A boom of thunder blasted across the sky. We all jumped and bumped our heads on the deck above.

"Ow!" they both complained, but fell silent as I told them what Monroe had told me, leaving out the whole part about Monroe, of course.

"Do you know where Amelia lives?" I asked.

"Of course we do," said Rome excitedly. "She's right around the corner from us!" Rome shook his head and smiled. "All this time and Faith was just a hop, skip, and pounce away. At least she's in good hands, but I know she'd much rather be home."

"I agree," said Alf, and the two looked at each in disbelief.

I was also in shock. They actually had agreed on something.

"Where's the house?" I asked.

"It's on Main Walk," replied Rome impatiently. "Near the Post Office. Let's go!"

"Yes, let's," said Alf.

I'd never been farther than Aeon Walk. I had just gone into the woods that day, stretching out into new territory, but since we knew Faith was safe and sound, couldn't we just wait until tomorrow morning? Main Walk sounded like it was far away and a storm was coming. Maggie said so. Monroe said so.

"Storm's comin'," I said. "Maybe we could—"

"No way, no how!" meowed Rome. "We can beat the storm."

"Yes," said Alf, "we can if we go now and stop talking."

"For once I will stop talking," Rome laughed.

The two of them ran out from under the house faster than a kitten can catch her tail.

I was Lily, the one who's name came first in our Pride. I had to go, but why wouldn't my legs move?

7

SAVING FAITH

✦

*Saving a dog
is a curious thing.
It makes one cat cry
and another one sing.*

As daylight edges away from the ocean and the bay, most days in the Grove end with a rosy sunset that welcomes the night. This was not one of those nights. The sky was darker than it should be and the wind blew through the pine and holly trees, sending prickly leaves down on our heads and under our paws.

Peter rushed by carrying his two dogs, Eva and Tinkerbell, who were both pleading for him to go faster. Two-leggeds hurried along on different walks, dashing into their homes, closing windows and doors. They knew what was coming.

Every living thing knew it, and here we were, probably the only ones crazy enough to be out in it.

A crash of thunder made us jump, and the swirling air made our tails go thump. A crack of lightening was so bright that we all jumped in fright.

Jean Skinner, the mail lady, hurried by faster than I had ever seen the old two-legged go before. One hand held her yellow rainhat on her head, the other pumped back and forth with each quick stride.

Sugar ran by us and yelled, "It's going to storm!"

"We know!" we hollered.

Cliff scurried up a tree and then from branch to branch over our heads. "It's going to storm!" he yelled.

"We know!" we hollered.

A twig fell on top of my head. "Hey!"

"Keep going!" shouted Rome over another clap of lightning and thunder. "We're almost there!"

Latifah and Redboy fluttered by right over our heads and started to chirp, "It's going to—"

"—we know!" we hollered before they could finish.

Seagulls squawked, crows crowed, sparrows fought the gale that was quickly growing, and I knew that somewhere Redboy and Latifah were going to bed, safely snug in their nest. Sugar would hunker down with her friends in the woods. Monroe was in his home with his family in the dunes. Cliff would be comfy in his hole in the tree. I wanted to be snug with Susan and Nancy, and even Spike. That would have to come later, though.

Our paws padded down Bayview Walk and I realized that we had already passed Aeon Walk. Like the woods, this was all new to me. New homes, new trees, new walks.

The first drop hit me, and then the next, and like a sudden ocean wave being dropped from the sky, the rain came. The wind blew water at us from all sides. Something very hefty flew over our heads.

"Trashcan!" yelled Alf.

Something else whizzed by my head, barely missing me.

"Trashcan lid!" hollered Rome.

I watched the lid fly in the air and vanish over a fence.

A broom rolled swiftly towards us as if sweeping up the fallen debris. We all jumped just in time. Branches fell, leaves ripped across our fur, and we got wetter and wetter and wetter until we were as soppy as three sponges in a stopped sink.

"We're wet!" I yelled.

"Yep!" bellowed Alf.

"She certainly has the gift for the obvious!" Rome shouted.

Lightning crackled, thunder boom-boomed in our ears, wind and storm raged all around us.

Alf piped up, "Not far now!"

Lightning, thunder, rain, and wind all did their best to stop us from reaching Amelia's house, but nothing can stop three determined, stubborn cats.

"This is it!" cried Alf and Rome. "This is Amelia's house!"

The next crack of lightning and thunder was so close, right over our heads, that my ears buzzed and all my hair stood up on end. My whole body was big tail. I felt like I did when I licked one of the electrical sockets in our house when I was only a very, very teeny kitty.

All three of us scratched at the front door and screamed for Faith, but the rain and thunder were so loud, I don't think any living thing, two or four-legged would have ever heard us.

"Let's go around to the back door!" shouted Rome.

We sprinted along the side of the house, slipping and sliding, and turned the corner. There were two large sliding glass doors closed up tight, and in a flash of lightning, we saw that we had indeed found Faith.

She lay shivering in the dark by the door. Rome and Alf meowed as loud as they could, "Faith!", and in another flash and crash of lightning, Faith looked up and saw the three of us at the door.

"Oh, Faith!" screamed Rome. "Oh, look at her, Alf, all alone and scared!"

"Alf, Rome!" Faith barked. "And ..." She cocked her head at me.

"I'm Lily!" I yelled then asked, "Where's Amelia?"

"She went out a while ago," Faith replied.

"Let us in!" shouted Alf and Rome.

"Let me out!" Faith yowled.

We all scratched at the glass door. Glass is such a strange thing for us four-leggeds to understand, almost as strange as doorknobs.

"We're getting no place fast," I yelled above another roar of thunder.

Crickle-crackle-boom-boom! The sound sent us flying in the air, but I suddenly saw a window in the living room that was half open.

"What do we do?" asked Rome. "Think! Think!"

"Follow me!" I hollered. I had a plan, a good one that I thought might just work.

The pile of firewood underneath the window I had seen on the way around the house had given me hope. I told Alf and Rome what we were going to do. They agreed and then we did it.

 I climbed up the stack of wood and jumped onto the windowsill. Alf and Rome joined me and together we pushed with all our might against the screen. With a pop, a few surprised meows and a crash, we were inside, and Faith was licking Alf and Rome. *Yuck.*

"We saved our Faith!" rejoiced Rome.

"Yes," said Alf, "but who's going to save us?" He looked up at the open window, at Faith, and then lastly at me.

"She can't jump very high, can she?" I asked.

Alf rolled his eyes. "Didn't quite think about that, did you?"

"Now, Alf," said Rome, "we got in, so we can most certainly get out. We're all smart kitties, and we've got one smart dog here, right Faith?"

Faith barked, "Yep! How about the door?"

Alf raised one eye and narrowed the other. "Have you ever heard of thumbs?"

"No," said Faith.

"Two-leggeds have them on their paws, or what they call their hands. The biggest, fattest finger that lets them do things we can't, like turning a doorknob is called a thumb. Our paws are thumbless and hopeless."

Hmm, I thought. No thumbs, no open door. But we had three cats, a dog, and sixteen paws between us all. We had a chance.

"We're going to open that door," I said in my most confident voice, my leader of the Pride voice.

Alf laughed. Rome and Faith both cocked their heads, almost amused by my confidence.

"If we can jump high enough to get to the doorknob," I said, "but the problem has always been holding on long enough."

Alf licked at his wet coat. "And how do you suppose we do that?"

"I'll tell you how," I said.

8

THE GREAT ESCAPE

✦

A great escape,
in thunder and rain,
makes a four-legged happy
to get home again.

A few moments later Faith was standing next to the door, right under the doorknob.

"Alf, you're next," I said.

"This'll never work," he complained.

"Get up there right now," Rome commanded.

"All right, all right." Alf climbed up on Faith's back and steadied himself the best he could. "This is a bit awkward."

"You're doing fine," I said. "Great job, Alf."

"Thanks, Lily."

I didn't have to tell Rome what to do. Besides me, he was the next lightest cat. The three of them teetered back and forth while Faith's nails clacked on the floor. "Whoa!" they cried, swaying like a piece of bamboo in the wind. I thought for sure they were going to topple over.

"Lean against the door!" I meowed.

They braced themselves against the door, leaning their sides into it, and that seemed to work. Once they had settled down, I slowly, carefully, climbed up Faith's and then Alf's leg.

"Hey!" Alf yelled. "Careful with those claws!"

I finally made it up onto Rome's back. The doorknob was right in front of my nose. *Purrfect*, I thought.

I carefully reached up with two paws, and tried to turn the knob one way and then the other, but it didn't want to twist. I had a clumsy time keeping my paws on the slippery knob. In a flash of lightning I saw my wet, gritty reflection in it. I thought, *I'm not going to be a kitty for much longer. I'm going to be a cat.*

"How's it going?" yelled Rome from below.

"It doesn't want to turn!" I shouted back.

Alf said encouragingly, "Keep trying, Lily, you can do it."

Right then, louder than anything I'd ever heard, a flash of lightning followed by an instant bang shook the house from the chimney all the way down to the thick round wooden piles that anchored the house into the island sand.

On the boom of the thunder, Faith was the first to fall over, followed by Alf then Rome. As I hung onto the doorknob my body swung back and forth. Suddenly, quietly, like a flower being plucked from the garden, the doorknob turned, clicked, and the door slid open a narrow crack.

I dropped to the floor and turned to Alf.

"No thumbs," he laughed, shaking his head.

Rome and Faith bounced around the floor. They meowed and barked and were so excited that they didn't notice how close they were to the door. With a quick bump from his rear end, Rome hit the door, closing it once again.

"Oops," he peeped like a mouse.

"I guess the first time was practice," growled Alf.

After opening the door the second time we all walked out, back into the storm, which didn't seem as bad as it had been before.

9

HOME AGAIN HOME AGAIN JIGGEDY JIG

✦

Home is a place,
that I love to be,
come rain or shine,
it's you and me.

As we trotted down the walk, the most amazing thing happened—the storm passed and a full moon shone over our heads, lighting our path home to a house called *Sunset Boulevard* that Alf, Rome, and Faith called home.

"I guess cats and dogs can get along," I said as I watched the three of them stroll happily in the moonlight.

"We don't always get along, Lily," called Alf.

"Nothing's *purrfect*," Rome said.

"I know one thing that's *purrfect*," said Faith.

"What?" I asked.

"Cherry Grove."

That's something all four-leggeds and wing*eds* could agree on: cats, dogs, cardinals, squirrels, raccoons, deer, snakes, bugs, chipmunks, even bluejays. You name it.

The three friends stood outside the black iron gate.

Rome sighed and said, "Home again, home again, jiggedy-jig."

We said our good-byes and then one by one they each walked through the little swinging door at the bottom of the back-door, into their home the way it was meant to be.

I very much wanted to go to my own home and when I got there, Susan and Nancy were waiting, as if they knew I was coming.

"Where were you Baby Cat?" they asked. "We were worried."

"Oh," I meowed, "here, there, everywhere."

And then we all curled up with Spike on the bed and drifted off into that place that every creature calls dreamland.

Yes, dogs were nice, cats were interesting, but I was very happy with my family, just the way it was.

10

FAMILY REUNION

✦

A family's a blessing,
if you can see it,
it's loving and caring,
I really do mean it.

A few days later I happened to go over to Sunset Boulevard to check in on the boys and Faith when Denise came home. We welcomed her with meows and barks, licks and gentle nudges.

"What are you doing here Faith?" she asked. "You're supposed to be at—"

Suddenly the phone rang.

Denise stared at us with an amusingly confused look on her face. She scratched her head then answered the phone.

"Hello? Oh, hi Amelia, I was just going to call you. No, well, she's right here with Alf and Rome, and Lily, too. Thanks so much for bringing her back over. You didn't? No, no, Faith couldn't have jumped up that high to your window. Well if you were over at Lynne's house during the storm, how in the world did Faith get here?"

Denise turned towards the four of us and narrowed her eyes. She grinned and shrugged her shoulders. "I don't know what these four have been up to, but I don't think we'll ever know."

11

THE PUNCHLINE

◆

A joke is something,
that can make you mad,
or lift your heart,
and make you glad.

On the way back home I passed Jimmy with his moms, Lucy and Diane.

"Wanna play, Lily?" Jimmy asked happily, his tongue hanging out.

"Maybe later," I said. I didn't think I was ready for that yet. I'd have to get to know him a little better. I also really wanted my morning nap under the bench on the deck.

Once I was home, I stretched out under the bench and heard the sound I disliked the most in Cherry Grove.

"Hey Carm, why did the cat run away from the tree?"

"I don't know, Tony, why *did* the cat run away from the tree?"

"She was afraid of its *bark*!"

They cackled. They laughed. My ears lay flat against my head. I'll tell you one day about cat's ears and what they're saying.

Yes, dogs and cats might get along sometimes, but cats and blue jays on the other paw ... never! I'd bet three whiskers on that.

ABOUT THE AUTHORS

Tim Steffen

Tim has been an apple picker, waiter, bartender, filmmaker, café owner, dog walker, Ragtime piano player, and newspaper reporter. He currently concentrates his time on teaching second grade at a private school in New York City, writing and illustrating children's books, and traveling. His work can be viewed at www.timsteffen.com.

Susan Ann Thornton

Susan is a painter, photographer, and digital artist. She has shown in one-woman and group shows around the country. She has also been an art teacher. Susan lives between homes in Cherry Grove and Santa Fe with Nancy, Spike, and "The Baby Cat", Lily. To view Susan's digital work visit www.suze-arts.com.

AUTHORS' NOTE

We hope you enjoyed reading *Saving Faith*, the second book in the Baby Cat Series. If you'd like to read about Lily's first exciting adventure, you can purchase the first book, *Home*

Sweet Home at www.baby-cat.com. On our site you can also listen to Susan sing the Baby Cat Song. And if you'd like to keep abreast of Baby Cat news and view video clips of the *real* Baby Cat who inspired this series, click on the link for our blog or go directly to it at: www.babycatadventures.blogspot.com.

Meow!

BABY CAT 3 COMING IN 2008!

978-0-595-46844-7
0-595-46844-6

Printed in the United States
92684LV00002B/1-99/A